Sue Likes Blue

Written by
Barbara Gregorich
Illustrated by
Joyce John

Sue likes blue.
What can we do with Sue?

She wants blue dresses.
She wants blue hats.

She has blue boots.
She has blue toys.

She likes blue cakes.
Blue cakes are hard to make.

Sue wants blue water.
Sue wants blue soap.

Sue has a blue bed.
Sue has blue blankets.

What can we do with Sue?
She wants everything blue.

This is what we will do.
We will give her blue.

Here, Sue. Paint with blue.
Blue, blue, blue.

Here, Sue. Here is blue paper.
Here is blue glue.

Look, Sue. See the blue dish.
See the blue food!

Stop! There is too much blue.

Everything should not be blue.
What should I do?

I know!
I will keep some things blue.
But I will use other colors, too!

And that is true.